GOES BANANAS

WALT DISNEY
PRODUCTIONS'

HERBIE

GOES BANANAS

A novel by
JOE CLARO

From the Walt Disney Productions' Film

Written by
DON TAIT

Based on characters created by
GORDON BUFORD

SCHOLASTIC BOOK SERVICES
NEW YORK • TORONTO • LONDON • AUCKLAND • SYDNEY • TOKYO

For Chris, Danielle, Noel,
Nicole and Tasha

ISBN 0-590-31609-5

12 11 10 9 8 7 6 5 4 3 2 1   5   0 1 2 3 4 5/8

Printed in the U.S.A.   01

Chapter
1

"**P**ort-o Val-lartah!" Pete read the signpost as they bounced along in the rickety old bus. "That's it, D.J.! We're almost there!"

"I can't believe it," D.J. said wearily. It seemed as if they'd been traveling forever.

Puerto Vallarta was a small Mexican town, and a sea resort much favored by American tourists. But Pete and D.J. hadn't traveled a thousand miles from Los Angeles just to enjoy its resort life. They'd come to see about a certain race car that was supposed to be garaged here.

Now, as the lurching bus creaked to a stop and they climbed stiffly out, D.J. wondered again why he'd let Pete talk him into this.

They stood by the bus, squinting in the hot sun. Pete looked happily at the sparkling ocean beyond the dock. Above it floated tourists from bright-colored parachutes, towed along by speeding boats.

"Puerto Vallarta goes on my list," he said.

"What list?" D.J. asked.

"My list of a hundred and one places to visit when I have money."

"Oh." D.J. collected their luggage and looked at the low buildings across the street. He saw a small town, and no garage in sight.

"It's still a mystery to me, Pete," he said. "Why would anyone want to *give* you a car that won the Monte Carlo Grand Prix?"

Pete sighed. He'd heard the same question too many times in the past few days. "You saw the letter," he said. "My uncle just doesn't want to sell it, for sentimental reasons."

"Yeah, but I wish I knew what your uncle considers a sentimental reason. A cracked engine block, for instance?"

"All we have to do is lay out the storage fee," Pete said. "We can't go wrong. Have you got the money?"

D.J. patted his back pocket. "Yes, I have the money," he whispered.

"Let's go get directions," Pete said. He started walking, and D.J. followed.

When they crossed the street, they were stopped by a ten-year-old boy, who planted himself in front of them.

"Shine, Mister?" the boy said, smiling. "Paco gives the best shine in town."

"No, thanks," Pete said, looking in the direction of some stores.

"Then how about a guided tour of Puerto Vallarta?" the boy said.

"No, thanks, son," Pete said. "We don't have the money for fun. Not this trip, anyway."

"Okay," Paco said. "Where you want to go? Paco will show you, free — on the house."

Pete looked down at the grinning face and grinned back. Then he took a letter from his pocket and read aloud.

"Perfecto Mecánico," he said. "On Avenida Cardinas."

"No problem," Paco said. "I show you exactly."

He ran to the sidewalk and pushed his shoeshine kit inside a doorway. Then he ran back to join his two new friends. He stood between them, put his arms around their waists, and gently guided them down the street.

"You Americans? I like Americans. They are very smart people. Some day I will go to America."

D.J. smiled for the first time. "When you come, Paco, look up Pete Stanchek here. He'll give you a place to sleep and show you the best ice cream parlors in town."

Pete shot an unfriendly look at D.J. They reached an intersection, and Paco pointed to their left.

"Down there," Paco said. "That's Avenue Cardinas. Turn left, go two blocks, and you will see Perfecto Mecánico."

Pete took a quarter from his pocket and held it out to Paco. "Thanks, young fella," he said.

Paco waved off the tip and said, "No. Welcome to Puerto Vallarta."

With a smile of surprise, D.J. said, *"Gracias, amigo."*

Paco shook hands with both of them. "See you later, alligator," he said. Then he ran back to where he stowed his shoeshine kit.

As they watched him go, D.J. said, "Cute

kid. Polite, helpful. Didn't have his hand out."

"Mmm," Pete said. "Come on. Down this street."

Their way to the mechanic's shop took them past the entrance of a certain hotel; it was bustling with tourists. Pete and D.J. hardly gave it a glance, but perhaps that was a mistake. Because some of its guests weren't tourists. They were there on business, very serious, even deadly business—like the people in room 714.

There were three men in that room. They were looking at a large photograph of a jungle area; it had been taken from a plane.

Shepard, the pilot who had taken the photo, was watching the reactions of the other two men. *He* knew what it showed. *They* were just finding out.

Prindle, a big hulk of a man, leaned over the table, staring at the photo. He had agreed to let Shepard come to his hotel room only because Shepard had once done him a very large favor. The favor involved transporting certain goods from South America to California without letting the government know about it.

Quinn stood nervously looking first at the photo, then at his boss. He knew what the photo showed. But he wasn't sure what his boss was going to do about it.

"It's that light area in the lower right-hand corner," Shepard said.

"Yes," Prindle said. "And you think that's the remains of an Incan village?"

Shepard smiled slightly. "You're the expert, Mr. Prindle. You tell me."

Prindle straightened up and faced Shepard. "Who else knows about this?" he asked.

"No one," Shepard said. "They were looking for oil, not gold. I'm the only one who flew over this area."

"And where is 'this area'?" Prindle asked.

"It's somewhere in South America," Shepard said, smiling. "And until you commit yourself, that's all you're going to know."

"It may *be* an undiscovered Inca city," Prindle said. "It may mean there's gold. So what do you want from me?"

"Cash," Shepard said. "And plenty of it. The risk here is enormous. If they catch you taking this stuff, they lock you up and throw away the key."

Quinn had a worried look on his face. "He's right, Mr. Prindle," he said. "This is national treasure you're talking about."

Still facing Shepard, Prindle said, "Quinn, if you'd like to seek other employment, you can begin right now." Silence. He spoke to

Shepard. "Is there another print of this?"

"No."

"Meet us in Quito in two days."

Shepard put the photo in his wallet as Prindle poured three glasses of wine.

"There has to be some mistake," Pete said.

"No mistake, Señor," the garage owner said. "That is the car Señor Douglas left with us."

He pointed to a corner where a sad-looking, battered Volkswagen bug sat staring at them. The racing stripe on its side and the number 53 on its roof hinted at some past glory.

D.J. said, *That thing* won the Monte Carlo Grand Prix?"

"That is what Señor Douglas told me," the owner said, shrugging. "And he would have won the Baja race too. But his girl, Giselle, she could not make the curve. So Herbie stopped and did not finish the race."

Pete and D.J. looked at each other with raised eyebrows. Was this man playing with a full deck?

"I know what you are thinking," the owner said. "But that is what Señor Douglas told me. Could I tell him he was crazy? No, he is a customer, and a friend. So I tell him I will take

7

good care of the car, until you come to pay for the storage."

Pete took a deep breath and let it out slowly. He walked over to the car and climbed into the driver's seat. He turned the engine on and gunned it a few times, while D.J. listened.

"Well?" Pete said.

"So it runs," D.J. said. "That's not going to make Mario Andretti very nervous."

"Let's take it," Pete said. "If nothing else, it'll get us home."

He turned off the engine and got out. As the garage owner wrote out a receipt, D.J. reached into his back pocket. The look of horror on his face immediately told Pete that their money was gone.

Thinking fast, and keeping his voice calm, Pete spoke to the owner. "Do you mind if we drive it once around the block first?"

The owner was reluctant, but this *was* Señor Douglas's nephew, after all. He agreed. Pete and D.J. calmly got into the car and slowly drove out of the garage. Then they peeled out in the direction of the bus depot.

"Cute kid!" Pete yelled. "Doesn't have his hand out! How could he have it out, when it was in your pocket! Let's find that little thief!"

They raced past the hotel, thinking only

about getting back to the bus depot. They didn't notice the three men leaving. Two of them wore business suits and carried suitcases. The third wore sunglasses and a windbreaker and carried an overnight kit.

As Pete and D.J. rounded the corner, a smiling ten-year-old boy approached the three men.

"Carry your bags, sir?" he said.

They ignored him, but he managed to get himself tangled among the three of them. The man with the sunglasses almost lost his balance trying to avoid the boy. The boy grabbed onto the man's waist to keep from falling. Then the man pushed him roughly aside.

The boy slipped something inside his shirt. He got up, brushed himself off, and trotted away, unnoticed by the three men.

He turned into an alley and took Shepard's wallet from inside his shirt. Grinning, Paco stuffed the wallet into his pocket.

Chapter
2

As Pete eased the VW down the avenue, he and D.J. scanned both sides of the street for Paco. It was a slow process, because any sign of movement was enough to make Pete slow down for a longer look.

Two blocks further down, Paco sat in an alley between two packing crates. The contents of both wallets were laid out on the bricks in front of him. He took a dollar bill from

D.J.'s wallet and stuffed it into his shirt pocket. Then he did the same with a dollar bill from Shepard's wallet.

This was all he wanted. Paco never stole more than he needed to get through the day. He took his time replacing the contents of each wallet. He always got a kick out of the bright, shiny credit cards Americans carried in their wallets.

"Stop!" D.J. whispered. Pete slammed his foot on the brake, and D.J. pointed into the alley. "There's a grubby little foot sticking out in there. My bet is that it's attached to Paco the Pickpocket."

Paco was running his fingers along the raised numbers of a credit card when he heard a squeaky car door being opened. He had no time to find out what it was. He started jamming stuff into the wallets, without worrying about which stuff belonged in which wallet. He stuffed the wallets inside his shirt, leaped up, and dashed to the back of the alley.

"There he is!" D.J. yelled.

Paco was already over the seven-foot fence at the back of the alley. When Pete and D.J. vaulted the same fence, they could see him disappearing along the side of a facing building on the next block.

D.J. followed him, and Pete sprinted for the other side of the building. When they reached the street, D.J. turned left, Pete turned right, and they wound up in each other's arms.

"I don't dance," Pete said, pushing D.J. away. "Where did he go?"

"There!" D.J. said, pointing behind Pete. Paco was already a block away and moving faster than the bus that had taken them into town. They took off in his direction.

Prindle and Quinn got into their taxi. Shepard leaned over and talked through the open window.

"Maybe you better take my card," Shepard said. "In case you have to get in touch with me."

He reached into his back pocket. Quinn and Prindle watched his eyes widen and his mouth drop open.

"My wallet!" Shepard yelled. "It's gone!"

"That little kid!" Prindle said, as he and Quinn climbed out of the cab. "Get back in that cab!" he screamed to Quinn. "Go get the police!"

Quinn got in, and the cab pulled away. Shepard ran down the street, and Prindle followed him.

* * *

Three blocks away, D.J. and Pete stood in the middle of an intersection.

"Where did he go?" Pete said.

Paco had lost them in the park. He had run along the beach for a few blocks, then doubled back through the park. He had no idea where Pete and D.J. were by now, but he didn't much care either. This was his territory. He could lose them any time he wanted.

He stepped out of an alley and spotted the mailbox on the corner. The mailbox was his usual way of returning borrowed wallets, once he had removed his small "finder's fee."

He walked calmly toward the mailbox. Just before he got to it, he reached inside his shirt and took out D.J.'s wallet. He stepped up to the mailbox.

D.J. stepped out of a doorway and grabbed Paco's wrist with one hand and the wallet with the other. Pete stepped out after D.J.

D.J. glared down at him. A dollar bill was sticking out of Paco's pocket. D.J. grabbed it and held it in front of Paco's face.

"Is this yours, little boy?"

"No," Paco said angrily.

"Is it mine?"

"*Si*," he said quietly, lowering his eyes.

D.J. thumbed through the wallet, then said to Pete, "Looks like that's all he took."

Paco watched them walk away. When they were out of sight, he took the other wallet from inside his shirt. Then he heard voices.

He turned and saw two men running down the street, screaming and pointing at him. He dropped the wallet into the mailbox, took off like a shot, and disappeared around a corner.

Prindle and Shepard stopped at the mailbox, completely out of breath.

"I think what we want is in there," Shepard said, pointing to the mailbox.

"Maybe," Prindle said. "Maybe not. We better find him."

Paco could handle himself on his own territory, but this was getting ridiculous. First the two young Americans catch him and take his dollar from him. Then the two screaming men from the hotel come chasing after him.

Trying to get away from them, he almost ran into a taxi that carried another man who started screaming at him. Behind the taxi was a police car. The three policemen had wanted Paco for a long time.

Paco could weave in and out of moving traffic with the best of them, and he had little trouble putting some distance between himself and his pursuers. But now two more cars full of policemen had joined the chase, and the pursuers were coming from every direction.

Paco's weaving caused several cars to stop short in the middle of the street. The policemen and the three screaming Americans had stopped several more cars. The main street of the little town suddenly looked like a highway in rush hour.

With the drivers honking their horns, the policemen blowing their whistles, and everybody else yelling, Paco was in a panic. He rounded a corner, aware of yelling from at least three different directions.

Paco didn't notice the empty VW that stood facing him at the end of the block. He did see a large cardboard box in front of a store, though. He jumped inside and pulled the top over him.

As several policemen ran past the box, the VW slowly started moving along the curb. No one noticed that it had no driver. A block away, Pete and D.J. were trying to find the spot where they'd left their car.

The VW pulled up to the cardboard box. Through all the noise, no one except Paco heard a soft beep come from the driverless car. He raised the top of the box slightly.

He stared at the car, which was flapping its front hood up and down. Paco accepted the invitation. He slipped out of the box and into the trunk, unnoticed. The trunk quietly closed. A few seconds later, D.J. and Pete came up to the car and got in.

"I thought we left it back there near the alley," D.J. said.

"I forgot to put on the emergency brake," Pete said. "It must have rolled. Let's just go pay the bill and get out of here."

Pete eased the car into a side street to avoid the traffic jam. As he was turning the corner, the hood lifted slightly. Paco stared across the street, right into Prindle's face.

"There he is!" Prindle yelled. "The kid is in that car."

Prindle, Shepard, Quinn, and half a dozen policemen ran into the path of the car. Its motor roared, and it zoomed in their direction. They all jumped to the sidewalk for safety and watched it burn past them.

Pete and D.J. sat plastered to their seats. "Hey, Leadfoot!" D.J. yelled. "You planning to sleep in the local jail?"

"I'm not doing anything!" Pete yelled back. "The car's driving itself!"

They came to a wider street. The car took

the turn on two wheels and then really tore out.

"Maybe this bug *did* win the Grand Prix!" D.J. said.

"I think we got ourselves a *car*!" Pete cried.

Back at the scene of the disaster, no one had tried to follow them. True, they didn't know anything about Herbie. They had no idea he'd won the Grand Prix without the aid of a driver. Nor did they know about the other astounding things Herbie had done. But they did know he was moving faster than anything they had available to chase him with.

With the help of a mailman, the police got Shepard's wallet from the mailbox and returned it to him. Two policemen watched as Shepard went through its contents.

"Is anything missing, Señor?" one policeman asked.

"No, no," Shepard said. "Everything's fine." From the look on his face, Prindle and Quinn could tell this wasn't true.

"We will continue to look for the car and the boy, of course," the policeman said. "Will you come with us to the police station?"

"We'll catch up with you," Prindle said quickly.

The policemen tipped their hats and walked off. Shepard waited until they were gone.

"The photo's gone!" he said in a furious whisper.

"Why would a kid like that take the photo?" Quinn asked.

"I don't know," Shepard said menacingly. "But we have to get it back. I'll never get another one."

"We'll get it back," Prindle said, staring in the direction Herbie had taken.

"I don't know who that kid is working for, but when I get my hands on him, he'll wish he'd never been born."

"Suppose the cops don't find him?" Shepard asked.

Prindle glared at him. "Forget the cops!" he said. "I've got my own people all over this area. Quinn, send the word out. I want that car!"

Chapter
3

The *S.S. Sun Princess* sat in the dock, its crew ready to set sail at any minute. One last-minute piece of cargo was holding them up, and they were working fast, anxious to get going.

Pete and D.J. stood watching as Herbie was carried overhead in a cargo sling. The captain of the *Sun Princess* stood on the deck tapping his foot. He was impatient to have this over with, so that he could get his cruise under way.

"Gently, boys!" D.J. called out. "That car's going to win the *Grande Premio do Brasil.*"

With Herbie on board, Pete and D.J. started up the ramp themselves. The ship's whistle warned them to hurry.

"D.J.," Pete said, "there's something weird about that car."

"I know," D.J. said, grinning. "It's dynamite! And it'll blow the doors off anything else in the race."

As they got aboard ship, Herbie was being lowered into the hold. His trunk opened slightly. Paco stuck his head out a little, saw where he was, and quickly retreated back into the trunk. Herbie's gentle beep was drowned out by the ship's second whistle.

As the ship pulled away from shore, a taxi screeched up and stopped at the dock. Prindle, Shepard, and Quinn hopped out and watched the *Sun Princess* floating away.

Quinn looked crushed by this development. "Now what?" he asked Prindle.

"Their first stop is Panama," Prindle said calmly. "We'll be waiting for them when they arrive."

"You sure you know what you're doing?" Shepard asked. "We can't be sure the kid got on the ship with the car."

"We can't be sure he didn't," Prindle said. "And we're not taking any chances. My people in town will keep an eye out for him here. If he turns up, they'll hold him for me. But I don't doubt that he's sailing into the sunset right this minute. Let's go."

Inside the cabin, the guests on the *Sun Princess* were getting ready for dinner. Melissa Davis was on her bunk, propped up on one elbow, reading a heavy textbook. Somewhere in the back of her mind, she knew it was almost dinner time, but she wanted to finish one more chapter.

Melissa was on this cruise as a guest of her Aunt Louise, who seemed determined to keep her niece from studying. Melissa had a Master's degree in Latin American Studies, and she was now working toward a Ph.D. This trip would give her a chance to get some first-hand information for her thesis.

Aunt Louise had other things in mind in arranging this cruise. Her general purpose, for both her niece and herself, was to meet *men*. Her own special goal was to meet A Man

— one who might qualify to become Husband Number 4.

Melissa had lately become one of Aunt Louise's minor obsessions. In her aunt's view, Melissa's priorities were all wrong. Postgraduate degrees were fine in their place, but they would never replace marriage.

Melissa often tried to explain that she felt *men* were fine in their place, but nothing was more important to her than her *doctorate*. Her arguments were so upsetting to her aunt that Melissa finally stopped trying to convince her.

She knew it was going to be hard to do on this cruise. But Aunt Louise had insisted on paying for her niece, and Melissa, who wanted to go, would never have been able to afford the trip on her own.

So here she was, trying to rush her way through a chapter before being forced to go out and socialize with her very social aunt. A knock on the cabin door told her she had run out of time.

"Come in," she called.

The door opened, and Aunt Louise glided in. She wore a shocking-pink silk dress, a pearl necklace, and matching earrings.

"Ah," she sang, closing the door behind her,

"there is nothing like an ocean cruise to revitalize one's senses."

When she caught sight of her niece propped up on the bed, her face fell. "Melissa, dear, when they say 'informal,' they don't mean an old cotton skirt! You aren't going to turn any heads in that!"

Melissa laughed, jumped off the bed, and looked at herself in the full-length mirror on her closet door. She was wearing a crisp summer skirt and a soft blouse. The mirror showed a pretty face without evening make-up, a pair of lively eyes, and a warm, wide smile.

"Turning heads isn't my style," Melissa said. "Anyway, they'll all be turned in your direction. You look terrific."

They walked down the corridor. Well, Melissa walked. Aunt Louise had a way of moving in public that suggested ballroom dancing more than walking.

"Melissa," she said, "there's a strange mystique about ships. One can *feel* romance pulsating in the air. A glance—a dance—a kiss in the moonlight — and some handsome young man has swept you off your feet!"

"My feet are fine where they are," Melissa said.

"Yes, stuck in the mud in sensible shoes!"

Melissa stopped walking. Aunt Louise stopped, glided in a half-circle, and faced her niece.

"Aunt Louise," Melissa said, as though talking to a child, "I really appreciate your taking me on this trip. I'm going to get some important material for my thesis. But that's all I'm looking for."

Aunt Louise pouted. "You don't have to wear blinders while you're looking," she said.

Then, brightening up, she added, "All right, all right. You do your thing, and I'll do mine. That is the way you young people say it, isn't it?"

Smiling, Melissa followed her to the entrance to the dining room.

Captain Blythe invited eight guests to eat at his table each night. The guest list was rotated, so that most of the passengers were given the honor at least once during each cruise.

Captain Blythe was a tall, middle-aged man who would have looked handsome in a coal-miner's outfit. In his uniform, he looked devastating. He had spent most of his life at sea, working his way up from lowly cabin boy to his present exalted position — commander of his own ship.

But Captain Blythe was not a happy man. He didn't fancy himself as the genial captain of a luxury cruise ship; his ideal was Captain Bligh, stern master of the *H.M.S. Bounty*. Captain Blythe still remembered the books he'd read as a boy — books about pirates, mutinies, British sea battles, and buried treasure. These days, a cruise ship was the best he could get; but he never fooled himself into believing it was the real thing. Half the time he thought he really was the captain of an old time British man-of-war.

As Melissa and Aunt Louise were being seated at their dinner table, the captain was "entertaining" his guests with sea stories. The chief steward stood by, nervously glancing at the captain and his guests. The chief steward had many duties on the *Sun Princess*. But the most important one was to keep his captain from making a complete idiot of himself in front of the passengers.

Through a mouthful of bread, Captain Blythe told his story. "The booty was taken aboard and the enemy vessel scuttled. Each captive seaman was given one hundred lashes, then spread-eagled on the rigging."

The captain smiled and chewed at the same time. The steward looked at the sickened faces of his dinner companions. He cleared his throat to get the captain's attention, but Blythe went on, unaware of their reactions.

"Believe me," he said cheerfully, "they didn't last long on those riggings. They were baked in the sun in no time at all. Mrs. Perkiss, try some of the green turtle soup. It's the chef's specialty."

Mrs. Perkiss closed her eyes at the mention of food and waved off the captain's suggestion. The chief steward's throat-clearing was beginning to sound like a struggling locomotive, but the captain ignored him.

Two tables away, Melissa was studying the menu, and Aunt Louise was studying the magnificent figure of the man who commanded the ship.

"Everything looks so tempting," Melissa said into her menu.

"Doesn't it?" Aunt Louise said, never taking her eyes off the captain.

By now, he was standing, acting out his story as he told it. The chief steward, getting hoarse from hinting, had turned beet red.

"As they clambered aboard," Blythe announced, "they were met with stiff resistance." He picked up a carving knife and struck a fencing pose with it. "It was thrust and parry!" he said, demonstrating with the knife.

The passengers stared open-mouthed, as Captain Blythe fought off a band of pirates with his carving knife. The chief steward had given up. He stood silently by, waiting for the worst. It came.

"The deck was awash with blood!" Blythe yelled, still fighting off the enemy. "Suddenly, the Commodore whirled —"

And the captain whirled, knife extended. The four guests nearest him ducked to avoid being beheaded. A lighted candle on the table was not so lucky, and the captain completed his whirl with the burning tip on the end of his knife.

The sight of the flame did what the chief steward had been trying to do for ten minutes. Blythe suddenly realized where he was, but he faltered for only a second. He immediately held the burning knife out to a passenger who had just taken out a cigarette. The man lit his cigarette, blew out the candle, and smiled weakly at the captain.

The captain sat at the table and smiled. "Pass the butter, please," he said.

Aunt Louise wanted nothing more than to run up and kiss him. But her attention was caught by a slight wave of the hand from the head waiter.

She had given him a small tip earlier in the day, together with instructions for choosing her dinner companions. When he caught her eye, he nodded in the direction of two young men waiting to be seated. She smiled at him, and he led them to her table.

"Well, this is a pleasant surprise," Aunt Louise said as they approached. "Two handsome young men as our dining companions. I'm Louise Trent, and this is my niece, Melissa."

"Hello, I'm Pete Stanchek, and this is Davey Johns."

As Pete and D.J. sat at the table, Aunt Louise asked, "Are you gentlemen going to Rio?"

"Not exactly, ma'am," Pete said, though he was looking at Melissa when he said it.

"I was just telling Melissa it's a city of romance," Aunt Louise said. "To get the most out of Rio, you really have to share it with someone. Wasn't I just saying that, honey?"

"I'm afraid I won't have time for that sort of thing," Melissa said, smiling politely. "I'll be using every minute I have getting material for my doctorate."

"You're going to be a doctor?" D.J. said, with just a trace of awe in his voice.

"Of Latin American cultures," Melissa said pleasantly.

Aunt Louise almost panicked at the direction the conversation might take. She decided to reroute it immediately.

"What takes you gentlemen to Rio?" she asked, glaring at Melissa.

"We're actually headed a little farther south," Pete said. "We're entering a car in the Brazil Grand Premio."

"Pete handles the wheel," D.J. said. "I'm the pit boss."

"You're a racing driver!" Aunt Louise squealed. "I just *love* race cars! Don't you, Melissa?"

"Not really," Melissa said.

They ate their shrimp cocktails in silence.

Below decks, it was dinner time for Armando, the crewman who was on watch in the hold. Carrying his dinner on a tray, he worked his way around tractors, bicycles, and huge packing crates. He had a favorite spot for eating dinner, an out-of-the-way corner where he wouldn't be disturbed.

The two crates were waiting for him, right

in front of the VW that had been carried into the hold at the last minute. He put his dinner tray on one crate and sat on the other. He removed the napkin cover and licked his lips at the chicken dinner that awaited him.

Then the phone rang, and he knew his treat would have to wait a little longer. He sighed, got up from his crate, and walked to the other side of a partition to answer the phone.

While Armando was gone, Herbie opened his hood just enough to let Paco look around. It was also enough for the aroma of the chicken dinner to drift under Paco's nose.

The hood opened a little more. Paco's hand reached out, grabbed the chicken, withdrew into the hood, then came out again, empty. This time, the hand removed the apple from Armando's dinner plate. The hand and apple disappeared, and the hood snapped shut.

Armando came back, sat down on the crate, and tucked his napkin inside his shirt. But the smile of anticipation faded when he looked down at his plate.

He looked around. He got up and looked along the floor. Then he got down on his knees and looked under the VW.

While he was down there, he heard a suspicious *clink*. He got up and looked at his plate.

A clean chicken bone had made an appearance.

While he stood there confused, Herbie's hood opened a few inches. A hand crept out and deposited another clean bone on the plate.

Armando crept over to the VW and bent his ear to the hood. He would recognize that sound anywhere. It was the sound of an apple being munched. His apple!

"Aha!" Armando cried, grabbing the handle of Herbie's hood. "So! You think you can steal my dinner and get away with it! We will see about that!"

He tugged at the hood. It wouldn't move. He angrily stomped over to a packing crate and picked up a crowbar. He turned to face Herbie, wielding his weapon as he came.

Armando stopped when Herbie's engine started up. He retreated when Herbie started moving. He ran to the phone after Herbie slowly moved past him.

"Number One Hold here!" Armando said into the phone. "Some of the cargo broke loose —or something! Send some help down here!"

Two other crew members had seen Herbie go by, and they came running up to Armando.

"Did you see that car?" one of them asked.

"Yes," Armando said. "Tell me, was anyone driving it?"

"No!"

An officer and five more crewmen came rushing down the stairs. Armando pointed behind them. They turned and saw Herbie pass through a doorway on his way to another part of the hold.

"Notify Captain Blythe!" the officer told Armando. "You other men follow me!"

Herbie picked up speed, zipping around pieces of farm equipment and large packing crates. His hood was open just enough for Paco to be able to see where they were going. But Paco wasn't looking. He had his head buried in his arms.

The sailors not only chased, they also yelled. They yelled loudest when they saw part of the cargo being destroyed.

Herbie was trying to be careful, but there wasn't much room in the hold. Every time he made a sharp turn, something or other would topple and fall behind him. The broken boxes and equipment were keeping the sailors far behind him.

Captain Blythe did not like being interrupted at dinner. He hated being interrupted when he was telling sea stories. He absolutely detested being interrupted while telling sea stories at dinner. Armando was frightened half to death.

"Am I to believe," Blythe screamed into the phone at his table, "that this car ate your chicken dinner?"

"Yes, Captain. And then he spit out the bones."

"Listen, man, do you have any idea of the penalty for drinking while on duty?"

"I have not been drinking, Captain. The car ate my apple too. I heard him with my own ears."

"I'll tell you what I'm going to do with your ears!" Blythe screamed.

The chief steward cleared his throat. The captain looked at him, then continued in a calmer voice.

"Where is the car now?"

"It went for a drive after dinner, sir."

"And was it smoking a cigar too?"

He slammed down the receiver. The chief steward cleared his throat, and the captain spoke to him.

"Whoever is behind this little jest," he said menacingly, "will receive fifty lashes before ship's company and be set adrift —"

The chief steward cleared his throat again, this time smiling at the guests. Blythe turned from him to the passengers at his table, his voice now dripping honey.

"Perhaps you'll be good enough to tell me about your grandson Snooky another time."

He turned, with fire in his eyes, and headed for the exit. The chief steward followed him into the hold, where the first person they came upon was Armando. The captain was about to order him boiled in oil, when an enormous crash interrupted his thoughts.

Fearing for his life, Armando pointed in the direction of Herbie's flight. The captain swiveled around and stormed off to see with his own eyes.

In the other part of the hold, four men stood on top of packing crates, draping a cargo net over a passageway. They watched silently as Herbie slowly came around a corner.

Herbie saw daylight and took off. His brakes screeched as a forklift cut off his path. As he came to a halt, the net was thrown over him. The net was tightened, and the crewmen cheered.

Captain Blythe stepped in front of Herbie just as his hood began to open. Paco stuck his head out and found himself staring into the fiercest face he had ever seen. Captain Blythe stared down at the little boy.

"Can fire really come out of a man's nose?" Paco wondered.

Chapter
4

Pete and D.J. stood—more or less at attention—in front of the desk in Captain Blythe's office. The captain stood staring out the porthole, his back to the two men. Next to him, the chief steward was referring to a written report, a summary of Herbie's latest adventure.

As he folded the report, he concluded, "And —uh—there was a little damage in the hold."

"Ha!" Blythe cried, spinning around and snatching the paper from the chief steward's hand.

"Ha!" he repeated, as he unfolded the report and read from it. "One crate broken glasses, $1,700! Two cases French wine, $483!"

"Some of that might be salvaged," the chief steward said meekly.

"Six birdbaths with cupids, $344!"

His eyes widened as he stared at the two men who had been called before him. He let the paper drop to his desk and he picked up a flogging whip.

"How did you want to handle that?" he asked slowly.

"Uh" — D.J. began — "uh — you mean *pay* for it?"

Through gritted teeth, the captain responded, "Did you plan to reassemble the stemware yourselves?"

Pete said, "But it isn't our respons — "

He was cut off by the crack of the whip on the desk. The chief steward made a motion in the captain's direction, but then thought better of it.

"I'll decide what is your responsibility!" the captain yelled. "I'm your captain! Aboard this ship, I'm your judge and jury!"

Heavy throat-clearing brought the captain back. Some of the redness drained from his face, but his eyes never left his two "prisoners."

"The cargo manifest," he said furiously, "states clearly that you, Peter Stanchek, are the owner of the car. *Your* car caused the damage, therefore — "

"Yeah," D.J. said, "but Pete wasn't driving the car."

The whip cracked again.

"I have been advised," the captain went on, "to be lenient with you two. Our public relations department suggests that I forget all charges of kidnapping and smuggling illegal aliens into a foreign country."

"You mean that kid?" Pete said angrily. "Where is he?"

"In the storeroom," the captain said, with a slight smirk. "Where he will remain until we reach Panama. At that time, he will be turned over to the authorities and returned to his native country. In the meantime," and now his voice was rising to its former angry pitch, "your automobile will be impounded until you have made good for all damages! Dismissed!"

Throat-clearing from the chief steward. Blythe shot him a look, looked back at D.J.

and Pete, and produced a large, artificial smile.

"I trust you have been enjoying the cruise so far," he said, with all the sincerity of a recorded announcement. "We have a shuffleboard tournament beginning at four bells. And there are disco lessons in the lounge. Beginners classes start at — "

"Thanks anyway," Pete said. He and D.J. turned and slumped out of the office. They walked down the corridor in silence for a while. Then D.J. had an inspiration.

"We could give the captain an I.O.U.," he said. "Then we'll pay him out of our winnings at the Grand Premio."

Pete looked over at him and sighed. "There is no way we're going to raise the kind of money he's looking for," he said. "Let's just chalk it up to experience. He keeps the car, and we work our way home."

D.J. wasn't about to give in that easily. "How about Aunt Louise?" he said. "Maybe she'll bail us out."

Pete wouldn't even look up for that one. "Dream on, friend," he said.

"No, wait," said D.J. He stopped walking, and Pete turned to face him. "She said she digs racing, right? And she does have plans for her niece."

"So?" Pete asked, confused. Then it dawned on him. "Oh, no."

"Don't say no," D.J. said. "All you have to do is keep Melissa enthralled with your tales of derring-do. While you're doing that, I'll introduce Aunt Louise to the delights of racing."

"I don't know," Pete said. "I don't like the feel of it."

"Nothing good comes easy," D.J. said, continuing down the corridor. "But even you can learn to turn on the charm a little."

The costume party that night was a huge success. D.J. kept wondering where all these people had managed to find such original costumes on board ship. Aunt Louise had to explain to him that they had all come prepared, that the costume party was a traditional part of the cruise.

D.J. and Pete, of course, hadn't come prepared for anything. So D.J. was costumed as an auto mechanic — bright orange overalls — and Pete was masquerading as a racing driver — bright silver jump suit.

There was no doubt about who was the star of the show. Captain Blythe, a patch over one eye, lit up the center of the dance hall in his British Naval Officer's uniform out of another century. When D.J. and Aunt Louise came in, the captain was holding court for a number of passengers, the ever-present chief steward ready, as always, to save him from himself.

"This suit is an exact replica," the captain announced, "down to the last button, of the uniform worn by Lord Nelson when he defeated the Spanish Armada." He struck a pose and added, "Seems like it belongs on me, doesn't it?"

Aunt Louise, in her Little Bo-Peep outfit, sidled up to him. "I like uniforms," she cooed. "They give a man — "

"At ease!" the captain barked.

Throat-clearing from the sidelines. The captain was back on Earth.

"Well," he said, "if you'll excuse me, I must circulate among the cargo—er—passengers."

His audience stared after him as he walked off. D.J. and Aunt Louise sat at a table, while Pete danced with Melissa.

D.J. continued the sales pitch he had started back at Aunt Louise's cabin, but she was only pretending to be listening. The fortunes of her niece on the dance floor were much more important to her.

"Like I was saying," D.J. said, "it's the thrill of a lifetime, watching your car streak across the finish line a winner."

"They seem to be enjoying themselves, don't they?" Aunt Louise said.

D.J. looked over at his friend and Melissa. She was wearing khaki pants, a matching shirt, and a pith helmet.

"Yeah," he said, "they're really hitting it off."

D.J. said it only because the plan called for Aunt Louise to believe that. He had no idea that it also happened to be true.

As they danced in each other's arms, Melissa leaned her head back and said, "Is this pith helmet bothering you?"

"Not a bit," Pete said, "I'm having a great time."

"Are you really?" she asked. "With all that's been happening?"

"Sure," Pete said. "Usually, when we race, it means towing a car across Texas in the middle of August, then bedding down in some fleabag hotel. Now here I am with soft lights, sweet music — and a pretty girl."

"Mr. Stanchek," she said smiling, "You don't have to say things like that."

"I know," Pete said. "You're different from other women I've known."

"I can well imagine." She laughed.

"I mean that as a compliment. For one thing, you don't giggle when there's nothing funny. You seem interested in what I have to say." He removed her hat. "And you *are* very pretty, Melissa."

From the other side of the hall, Aunt Louise beamed at them.

Three hours later, D.J. lay on his bunk with his hands behind his head and a big smile on his face. The door opened and slammed, but he continued smiling at the ceiling.

"Hello, Casanova," he said.

"This is the pits!" Pete said.

D.J. sat up on the bunk, his smile gone. "Did something go wrong?" he asked.

"You and I went wrong! I don't like playing games with people, especially nice ones."

"Come on, buddy," D.J. said, "just hang in there a few more days. Aunt Louise already gave me the check. The car is out of hock." Pete relaxed a little at this news. "And she said she'll sponsor us all the way. We name it, she buys it. All you have to do is keep making like Burt Reynolds."

"That's the deal?" Pete asked, flopping on the bunk.

"She didn't actually say it," D.J. said, "but I could read between the lines. We're back in the running, buddy-boy. Nothing is going to stop us now."

Now it was Pete's turn to stare at the ceiling. He'd need some time to convince himself that this wasn't all a pretty rotten trick to play on someone he liked.

The party was still going on, and the sounds of laughter and music drifted down to the hold. Herbie had been parked against a wall with heavy wooden blocks shoved up in front of his tires.

Armando would come to check on Herbie every hour or so, just to make sure the blocks were secure. He had just been in for his pre-dinner check, and he was now off eating somewhere.

Herbie's front wheels began to move slightly. The blocks were pushed in very tight, and he had to struggle. But soon, the wheels were moving a little more, then a little more. Finally one of the blocks slipped away. Once that happened, Herbie had more freedom, and the second block was soon gone.

He silently slipped out of his corner and rolled to another part of the hold. He stopped when he came to a wire mesh cage with a heavy padlock on its door. Paco was sound asleep inside the cage.

Herbie beeped softly. Paco stirred a little, but didn't open his eyes. Herbie beeped once more, and Paco turned over on his back. A third beep, and Paco opened his eyes.

"Hi," he said softly. He reached his fingers through the mesh and touched Herbie's front bumper. Then, remembering what they'd both been through, he smiled.

"The captain sure was mad, wasn't he?"

Beep, beep.

"What do you think they'll do with us?"

Beep.

"I don't know either. I guess they'll send me back where I live, with the orphans."

Beep.

"No, it isn't so bad. If it gets bad, I'll run away again. Can we be friends?"

Beep, beep, beep.

"Good. What's your name?"

Beep.

"What? Never mind. I'll just call you *Ocho*, okay?"

Beep beep.

By the time Armando finished his dinner, Herbie had already figured out how to get Paco out of that cage. Armando showed up for his inspection, but he stopped dead when he got near the board that held the keys.

He saw Herbie in front of the board. He saw Herbie's antenna bend forward and lift one of the keys from its hook. Then he saw Herbie silently go in the direction of the wire cage. He ran immediately for the phone.

Herbie delivered the key to Paco, who unlocked the padlock and stepped out of the cage. He was free for only a few seconds when he heard loud footsteps. They were getting louder very fast.

Herbie opened his driver's door. The driver's seat moved forward, and Paco slipped into the back seat. As soon as he hit the floor, the door closed, and Herbie took off, away from the approaching footsteps.

On the floor at the back of the car, Paco now heard voices added to the footsteps. The voices were not friendly.

Herbie raced around a corner and passed an open freight elevator. He slammed on his brakes, backed up, and moved into the elevator. Then his antenna bent forward and pressed one of the buttons. The elevator doors closed just before the sailors turned the corner.

Captain Blythe was surrounded by a group of women, who were amazed at his stories. Next to him, of course, was the chief steward.

"In those days," Blythe sang out, "a captain was a captain, and a ship was a ship. The only women aboard were kept prisoners in the hold."

The chief steward cleared his throat, but he felt this remark called for something a little more direct.

"The captain is having his jest with you, ladies," he said.

"I'm telling it like it was!" the captain retorted. Then, in a soft whisper to the steward, he added, "And the way it should still be."

He would have gone on—perhaps endlessly —except for a disturbance. From the kitchen came the sounds of crashing pots and pans and loud voices.

"What now?" Captain Blythe said, rolling his eyes toward the sky. The voices got louder, and he headed in the direction of the kitchen.

He stopped at the end of a long table covered with cakes and pastries. He stopped because of what he saw coming out of the kitchen.

That infernal VW had broken loose. It burst through the kitchen doors, carrying a passenger on its hood. The pastry chef, screaming and trying to keep his balance, held an enormous cream cake in the shape of a mermaid.

Herbie raced out of the kitchen and then stopped short at one end of the pastry table. From the other end, the captain watched as the pastry chef kept on going. The chef was tossed onto the table. The mermaid cake was tossed into the air.

Herbie's aim couldn't have been more accurate. The cake hit Blythe right in the face. He fumed. The passengers gasped.

"Beep," said Herbie. Then he flapped his hood a few times for emphasis.

Chapter
5

"**B**ut, Captain," Aunt Louise whined, "be reasonable!" He was marching down a corridor toward the stern of the ship. She was chasing after him.

"How could a *car* have let the boy out of that cage? Explain that!"

"I cannot explain it," he said calmly but firmly, "any more than I can explain the Bermuda Triangle. Nor do I intend to try."

His pace quickened, and so did hers. Her voice also rose in pitch a couple of notches.

"Captain, I appeal to you, as a woman!"

"I'm afraid you don't," he said. "My course is set. Nothing will make me change it."

When they reached the stairs, Captain Blythe continued to march, but Aunt Louise stopped and yelled down at him.

"I'm the sponsor of that car," she said. "And it's going to win the *Grande Premio do Brasil*."

He stopped in the middle of the stairway, turned, and smirked up at her.

"Madame," he jeered, "if you were to bring that off, I would not only part the Red Sea, I would tint it magenta."

Pleased with that remark, he turned and continued on his way. Sadly, slowly, Aunt Louise followed.

Outside, she came upon one of the most bizarre sights she had ever seen. Herbie was resting — upside-down — on two planks that extended beyond the rail of the ship. He was about to become the first motor vehicle ever to walk the plank.

The chief steward and several crewmen stood next to the upturned car, watching their captain approach. Other crew members stood nearby. At some distance, small knots of passengers watched the incredible scene. Aunt Louise joined D.J., Melissa, and Pete. Paco was off to one side, handcuffed to two burly guards.

The captain reached the car, surveyed his men, and nodded to the chief steward.

"Sir," the steward said meekly, "some of the passengers might not understand."

Blythe turned red. "Since when is a captain accountable to a pack of mutinous — " This time, he caught himself without having to hear a throat being cleared. He continued in a much milder tone, "I'm only abiding by the traditions of the sea."

Now he spoke to the assembled crew. "Ship's company, stand to, to witness punishment. By the powers vested in me as captain of this ship, I deem this vehicle a menace to life and limb. I herewith commit it to the sea."

Next to Herbie stood the drummer from the dance band. At a signal from the captain, he began a drum roll. At another signal, six crewmen bent to lift the planks under Herbie's roof.

"Pete," D.J. said, "can he really do this to our car?"

"Unless the Governor calls," Pete said. "I think he's about to."

"Well!" Aunt Louise said indignantly. "They shouldn't do it while the car is still alive!" Melissa, Pete, and D.J. looked nervously at her, but Paco sobbed, watching the crewmen raise the planks. Then he brightened when he heard Herbie's engine start up. He silently cheered as Herbie's wheels began to spin.

But there was nothing Herbie could do. His wheels spun around, his engine raced. But it was all in vain; he was helpless.

As the drum roll continued, the planks were lifted higher and higher. Herbie began to slide toward the sea.

Tears ran down Paco's face. He saw Herbie leave the planks, and he gasped as he heard the heavy splash. Then he—and everyone else —looked out at the wake of the ship. The drum roll had stopped. They were sailing away from the sinking car.

The *Sun Princess* had barely docked in Panama, when Pete and D.J. found themselves deposited on shore. To their surprise, Aunt Louise followed them down the gangplank.

"You too?" Pete asked.

"Lock, stock, and luggage," Aunt Louise

said. "Anyone even vaguely associated with that car is being put ashore. If it hadn't been for the chief steward, we'd have been right behind the car on those planks."

"I'm sorry it turned out this way," Pete said.

"Nothing to be sorry about," Aunt Louise said. "I'm the one who decided to get out of needlepoint and into racing."

"Actually," Pete said, "I was apologizing for more than that. See, we needed backing, so while D.J. was selling you on the car, I — "

"You," Aunt Louise said, smiling, "were trying to keep my niece occupied."

"You *knew* what we were doing?" D.J. asked.

"I was hoping," Aunt Louise said to Pete, "that something might develop between you and Melissa. She's really a wonderful girl."

"She is," Pete said quietly, "but not for somebody like me. That's why I told her all about it a while ago. I didn't want her to get hurt."

Melissa came down the gangplank with two suitcases. She kept her eyes forward as she strode between Pete and D.J.

"Sorry, boys," Aunt Louise said. She picked up her own luggage and followed her niece.

"Well," D.J. said, "how do you say, 'We need a job' in Spanish?"

They walked slowly away from the ship, having no idea what they should do. They passed several parked cars, not paying attention to any of them.

Three men sat in one of them, watching people come down the gangplank. They all tensed as they saw Paco being led down by a ship's officer.

"There he is!" Quinn said. "What do we do?"

"Let me handle it," Prindle said. All three got out of the car, walked to the gangplank, and confronted the officer.

"I don't know where you're taking this boy," Prindle said, "but I believe I have a prior claim on him."

The officer seemed relieved. "Are you from the Juvenile Authority?" he asked hopefully.

"Uh — yes," Prindle said.

Paco looked up for the first time, recognized Prindle, and shouted, "No, he isn't!"

Prindle had hoped it would be simple, and Paco's outburst got him angry. "You listen to me!" he said through clenched teeth.

Paco didn't know why these men would come all the way to Panama to get him. But he did recognize danger, and he wasn't about to hang around to find out what these men wanted.

He did two things almost simultaneously. He gave Prindle a swift punch in the stomach, and he kicked the officer in the shin.

With Prindle doubled over, and the officer hopping on one foot, Paco had the few seconds he needed. He ran in the direction of a passing truck.

"Stop that kid!" Prindle yelled.

But there was no one to stop him. The truck had an open back, and as it passed Paco, he hopped in. The last he saw of the dock was Prindle holding his stomach and the officer kneeling on one knee, nursing his bruised shin.

Paco got off the truck an hour later, when the driver stopped for something to eat. He wandered along a beach for a while and began to feel very hungry.

When he saw four men cooking fish over a fire on the beach, he knew what to do. He found a tree branch that would serve as a fishing pole. He borrowed some line from the men—they offered him food, but he wanted to catch his own. Then he went fishing from the end of a pier.

He sat for an hour without a bite. This didn't

discourage him, because he knew fishing could be a slow business. So he waited, staring out over the restless water.

Paco knew that staring for a long time could sometimes make you see things that weren't there. So he thought it was his imagination when he saw something bobbing up and down.

He stared a little longer, and saw it again. But this time, he knew that something was really there. And it was moving. It was shaped like a large rock. But large rocks don't float.

As it got closer, Paco began to hear a faint sound. As faint as it was, he would recognize that beep anywhere.

"Ocho!" he yelled.

It was Herbie, and he was floating toward shore. But Paco also saw that the car submerged itself and stayed under for a long time before bobbing up again.

"He's drowning!" Paco screamed.

He ran to the four men who had been eating on the beach. They were busy tarring the bottoms of two rowboats.

He saw a rope near the rowboats, grabbed it, and ran for the water.

"He's drowning!" Paco yelled. "Help me save him!"

One of the men ran to get a donkey. The

others stood on the beach and cheered Paco on.

He swam out to Herbie. The car had just come up from another long dip underwater. Paco tied the rope to the front bumper and began swimming to shore.

Two of the men waited, knee-deep in the water, for Paco. He was exhausted when he got to them. They grabbed the rope from him and ran it into shore. One of them tied it to the donkey. It took some doing, but Herbie was finally dragged onto the beach and out of the water.

They turned him right-side-up. Paco looked sadly at his friend, covered with mud, seaweed, and grime. He looked at the four men. All shook their heads sadly.

"What's the matter?" one of them asked. "It's an old wreck."

"He was my good friend," Paco said.

"Your *friend*," another man said, "is nothing but junk."

All four men laughed at this and went back to their work.

"I guess they're right, Ocho," Paco said bravely. "I will have to leave you here. I have to go because some guys are looking for me. *Adios, amigo.*"

He patted Herbie's hood, gave him one last

look, and turned to walk off. Three steps later, he stopped and listened. Herbie coughed.

Paco turned, his eyes wide. A smile was beginning to form. "Try it again, Ocho!"

Another cough. Then a sputter and a third cough. Paco ran back and jumped onto Herbie's hood.

"Come on, Ocho!" he said. You can do it!"

Cough, cough, sputter, cough.

"Atta boy, Ocho! Keep going!"

Sputter, cough, sputter. Then the most beautiful sound Paco had ever heard. Herbie's engine turned over.

"You did it!" Paco jumped off the hood, opened the driver's door, and climbed in.

"You did it, Ocho! You're alive!"

Herbie rolled slowly along the beach, testing his wheels. Everything seemed to be in working order. He picked up speed, and Paco cheered.

The four men watched in amazement, as Herbie "danced" in wider and wider circles on their beach.

"You feeling better now, Ocho?" Paco called out.

Beeeeeeeeeep!

How could a smart *race* car like Herbie fall into the drink? It's like this. . . .

D.J. (Charles Martin Smith) and Pete (Stephan Burns)
catch Paco (Joaquin Garay) with their wallet; Herbie
drives up to help Paco, who hides in his trunk.

Paco (inside Herbie) is hoisted aboard ship en route
to the Brazilian race. (below) In the hold, Paco steals
Amando's (Vito Scotti's) food. Amando thinks it's
Herbie, and chases him around the ship.

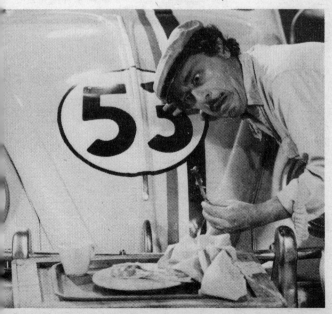

Mad Capt. Blythe (Harvey Korman) hears about Herbie and sentences him to drowning. (Paco is no longer inside Herbie.)

Lovely Melissa (Elyssa Davalos). (*below*) Her Aunt Louise (Cloris Leachman) adores Blythe, in a British Admiral's uniform at a ship's costume ball.

When everyone leaves the ship in Panama, Paco welcomes Herbie ashore, helps him dry out, and turns him into a taxi with some paint.

Herbie engages in bullfighting while Pete and Melissa
try to repair the bus that Melissa has bought for "wheels."

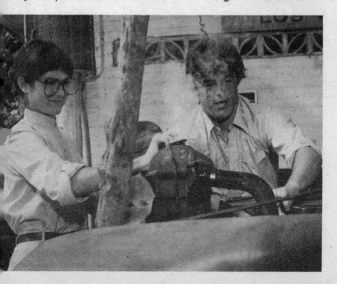

Blythe finds out his ship
has sailed without him.
(*below*) Pete and
Melissa find out they
really like each other.

Chapter
6

All Herbie wanted to do was ride, mostly to get that sea water out of his system. Paco sat back and enjoyed the beautiful view along the coast and the many small towns they rode through.

In one of these towns, Paco got Herbie to stop at a garage. Paco talked the owner into letting him have some paint.

He had Herbie pull into the garage, and then

he got to work. Paco was happy, confident that he had lost those three men forever. How could he know that a bright red VW riding through those small towns was an event that could never be kept quiet? How could he know that the three men were right now hot on his trail?

Paco finished his paint job and stood back to admire it. The word TAXI was painted on Herbie's door.

"You look good, Ocho, like a real taxi. Now we can make lots of money. Then Paco never have to steal nothing anymore."

Suddenly, a shadow appeared on Herbie's hood. Paco wheeled around and saw Prindle and Quinn blocking the doorway to the garage.

"You won't get away this time, kid," Prindle said. "So just relax."

Quinn stepped up to Paco, grabbed his arm, and twisted it.

"Where is it?" Prindle asked.

"Ow!" Paco screamed. "That hurts! Where is what?"

"The picture," Prindle said, as Quinn twisted the arm a little more. "It was in that wallet you took in Puerto Vallarta. It was missing when we got the wallet back. Where is it?"

"I don't know," Paco cried. "Maybe it got mixed up!"

Quinn raised his hand to slap Paco in the face. Prindle reached out and stopped him.

"What do you mean, *mixed up?*" Prindle asked.

"With the other man's wallet," Paco said.

"He's lying," Quinn said.

With a gesture, Prindle told Quinn to let go of the boy's arm. Then he put his face close to Paco's.

"Listen to me, boy," he said. "I want *you* to get that photo back. I don't care how you do it. Just get it! If you don't, *he's* going to cut this car of yours into little pieces."

A popping sound made Paco turn his head. He saw Quinn, grinning and holding out a flaming torch.

"You understand, kid?" Quinn said. "That car will be little metal strips that you can hang on your Christmas tree."

"*Si*," Paco whispered. "I understand."

Not far from where the *Sun Princess* was docked was a small restaurant — with a small kitchen. In this kitchen, two young *Norte-americanos* were washing and drying a pile of dishes. It was the only way they could get a meal from the owner.

"That car could have put us in the big time," D.J. said dreamily, as he sloshed a washcloth across a dish. "We could have been international celebrities."

"It was that kid!" Pete said angrily, as he reached for a clean dish to dry. "From the time we ran into that brat, *nothing* went right!"

"Hi, guys!" they heard. It wasn't possible! But there was no mistaking that high-pitched chirp. They whirled around in disbelief, and there was Paco.

"Speaking of four-foot crime waves," D.J. said.

"What do you want now?" Pete asked.

"I come to say I'm sorry if I make trouble for you," Paco said.

"Fine," Pete said, turning back to his pile of dishes. "Now get out of here,"

Paco began to sob. Pete turned back to see tears running down his face.

"I will go," Paco said. "I just want you not to be mad at me."

"All right, all right," Pete said. "Don't cry. Nobody's mad at you. What's done is done."

Paco timidly held out his hand. D.J. half smiled as he shook it. Then Paco was overcome with emotion. He threw his arms around D.J.'s waist. D.J. was a little embarrassed, but he returned the hug.

"I'm sorry," Paco said, backing away.

"No hard feelings, kid," D.J. said. Forget it."

"*Gracias.*"

"Gloriosky," Pete said, enjoying the soap opera scene. "It makes me feel warm all over."

Paco eased out of the doorway and ran. Pete and D.J. got back to work. Five seconds later, D.J. slapped his back pocket.

"He did it again!" he screamed.

They ran out the door and down the block.

"Come on back here, you little—" Pete and D.J. stopped dead when they saw Paco.

"That's our car!" D.J. yelled.

"How could it be?" Pete asked.

While they were wondering, Herbie and Paco made their getaway.

Prindle and Quinn were waiting outside their car a mile away. As Herbie came into view, they both waved him down. The car sailed right past them. They both got in their car to follow.

Herbie zipped down a wide street with very little traffic. Paco kept checking the rearview mirror for Prindle's car. So far, there was no danger of being caught.

Paco looked ahead and saw a policeman directing traffic at an intersection. "Better stop up ahead, Ocho," he said.

Herbie stopped at the corner. On the sidewalk to his right, Aunt Louise came out of a store, carrying several bulky packages.

"Taxi!" she called.

On the sidewalk to Herbie's left, Captain Blythe came out of an antique store, carrying an enormous model of an old ship.

"Taxi!" he called.

Both back doors opened at the same time. Both people were too busy with their packages to notice each other.

"Pier six," Captain Blythe ordered. "The *Sun Princess.*"

"Pier five," Aunt Louise said. "The *Windsong.*"

Captain Blythe lowered his model carefully to the seat, which gave him a clear view of his fellow passenger.

"YOU!" he sputtered. "I'm sorry, but I must return to my ship immediately! You can have the cab after that. Driver, pier six!"

In the sideview mirror, Paco could see Prindle's car approaching. He whispered to Herbie, "We're in real trouble, Ocho."

The policeman waved Herbie's line of traffic on. Herbie took a sharp right to get away from Prindle's car.

"I have prior claim on this taxi, Captain,"

Aunt Louise said firmly. "However, if you'll reconsider your order to banish us —"

"I *never* reconsider *anything*!"

With that, Blythe hunched himself toward his window—and saw that they were heading *away* from his ship.

"Driver!" he demanded. "Where do you think you're going?"

"*No comprendo, Señor,*" Paco said.

Something about that voice made the little hairs rise on the back of Captain Blythe's neck. He leaned forward to get a better view of the driver.

"YOU!" He turned to Aunt Louise, a look of total disbelief on his face. "It's that same kid!"

Aunt Louise began to smile. Then she looked around her.

"You think that's something?" she asked, laughing. "It seems to be the same car!"

Blythe realized this was true, and he panicked. "Let me out!" he yelled wildly. "Let me out right here, boy!"

"Can't stop now, Señor Captain," Paco said, watching the rearview mirror for signs of Prindle.

Blythe tried to open his door, but it wouldn't budge. As Herbie careened around a corner, Blythe was thrown up against his newly bought antique model; it crunched sickeningly.

He threw himself forward and pounded on his window.

"Help!" he screamed. "I'm being shanghaied!"

Aunt Louise's face was pressed against her window. Herbie came barreling down a narrow street just as Melissa stepped out of a store. As she watched the little red VW whiz by, she heard Captain Blythe's muffled cries for help. She also saw her aunt's frightened face, flattened against the window.

She stepped out into the street. The blare of a horn drove her back on the sidewalk, just in time. She was almost hit by Prindle's speeding car.

Pete and D.J. came running around a corner. They looked at Melissa, then off in the direction that held her interest. There they saw Herbie disappearing in the distance.

"It's that kid!" Pete said. "He robbed us again!"

"He's in the car!" Melissa said, pointing. "He's kidnapping Aunt Louise and Captain Blythe!"

Pete and D.J. looked at each other, eyes wide and mouths open.

"In our car," D.J. said.

Melissa wasn't going to waste time standing around with these two befuddled victims. She spotted a battered bus creaking its way along the avenue, and she ran out into the middle of the intersection. She began waving her arms at the driver, who had little trouble slowing down and stopping for her.

Pete wasn't so sure he trusted the brakes on the bus. He rushed out and tried to get her back on the sidewalk, but she wouldn't budge until the bus stopped.

"You pull enough stunts like this," he said, "and you'll never get to finish that thesis."

For a second, she forgot the crisis. She lowered her arms and smiled at him, grateful for his concern. Then she remembered her aunt, and the smile faded.

"What are you going to do?" Pete asked.

"The only thing I can do," she said. "I'm going to buy the bus."

Chapter
7

As Melissa ran around the side of the bus, the doors opened. She got on, but Pete and D.J. stood staring at each other.

"She didn't say what I think she said, did she?" Pete asked.

"I think she did," D.J. answered. They both followed Melissa into the bus, which had ten or twelve passengers.

"How much?" Melissa asked the driver.

"How far you want to go?"

"No, no," Melissa said impatiently. "How much for the bus?"

The driver looked confused, then grinned at her. "Well," he said, "let me see now. I have to be honest, lady. The bus is not brand new."

"I don't have time for understatements," she said. "How much?"

"Not brand new," he repeated, "but it does have two new tires." Melissa started rummaging through her purse. "And I changed the oil only last year. Or was it — "

"Never mind!" Melissa said. She had just added up what she had in her purse. "Is $342 enough?"

The driver's grin got broader. "You got yourself a bus, lady!" he said. Then he turned to the passengers and called, "Next bus, please!"

The passengers weren't happy about it, but there wasn't much they could do. Their driver had just sold his bus, and they had witnessed the transaction.

There was a lot of grumbling and muttering. There was some bumping of packages and pocketbooks, but soon the bus was empty.

The driver stepped out into the street, smiling at the wad of bills in his hand. He said, "It's best if you put in water every ten miles." Then he waved and trotted down the street to help his passengers flag down another bus.

Melissa made her way to the driver's seat, but Pete stood in front of her.

"Do you mind?" she asked coldly.

"Yes, I do," Pete said.

"It's my bus," Melissa said.

"I know, but this isn't any time for pride. I can handle it better than you. I practically drive for a living, remember?"

She considered this and looked at D.J. "He's right, Melissa," D.J. said. "This crate is in pretty bad shape. Let him take it."

She considered once more, then stepped back and took a seat. D.J. joined her, Pete got into the driver's seat, and they took off. The driver and his passengers waved good-bye as the bus passed them.

Miles outside of town, the bus noisily made its way along a lonely road. Its three passengers rocked in their seats, as though they hoped to propel it with their bodies.

Far, far in front of the bus, a black sedan traveled at top speed. The driver kept his eyes on the road. The other man in the car kept checking the sky for a small plane. Shepard was to pick them up as soon as they had gotten the photo from Paco.

Not very far ahead of the sedan, Herbie merrily led the race. Paco sat in the front seat, having the time of his life. Aunt Louise, though a little frightened, wasn't having a bad time herself.

Even Captain Blythe felt better. "Now hear this!" he boomed. "Release me this instant, or I will have you tied to a cannon to be discharged at sunset."

Paco turned his head and said, "I cannot stop, Señor Captain. Two men said they would cut up Ocho in little pieces for a Christmas tree. And two other men are very mad at me."

Back in the sedan, Quinn said, "We'll never catch that thing. I have it floored now!"

"Keep it floored!" Prindle said, looking for the plane. "He has to stop sometime."

In the bus, they had to yell to be heard. "Is that a new banging noise I hear?" Melissa shouted.

"No," Pete yelled back. "It's just louder. It might be getting ready to throw a rod!"

"Is that serious?"

"Not if it happens in front of a hotel!"

As they came into a small town, Herbie could see that the sedan was gaining on him. It was time to do something about it.

He made a left turn into a small street. He headed straight for the entrance to an arena.

Paco saw the sign and yelled, "No, no, Ocho! Not in there!"

It was too late. Herbie rode right into the bullring. Aunt Louise and Captain Blythe were both sitting back in their seats, paying little attention to where Herbie was taking them. It was the roar of the crowd that caught their attention.

"What was that?" the captain asked.

Paco answered, "Uh — we are at the bullfights, Señor Captain."

"Oh," Aunt Louise said, "this is exciting!"

"I think it will be, Señora," Paco said.

"What does he mean by that?" Captain Blythe asked her.

All they knew was that they were riding in a tunnel. Only Paco knew where this tunnel was going to lead them. The black sedan pulled up to the entrance and followed Herbie inside. That meant two more people were in for a surprise.

With the sedan on his tail, Herbie crashed through a barricade and came charging into the bullring. Once out in the open, he stopped short. The sedan stopped right behind him.

The crowd roared at this unexpected development. The bull halted in his rush toward the matador to study the cars. He took a few steps back.

The matador looked furious at this interruption of his performance. He waved his arms and yelled.

Prindle yelled too. "Let's get out of here!"

Quinn backed up the way he had come in, but two men had already closed the gates. Nobody was eager to have the bull charge into the tunnel.

The matador had given up. Disgusted, he tossed his cape into the air and walked off. The cape sailed down and landed on the sideview mirror of the sedan.

The bull seemed to believe that the show must go on, no matter what. The matador had tossed the cape to the sedan. All right then, he would perform with the sedan.

"Get the cape off the car!" Prindle screamed.

Quinn reached his hand out slowly and tried to grasp the cape in his fingers without exposing too much of himself. It was too late. The bull was already in mid-charge.

Quinn pulled his hand back in just as the bull's horns hit the side of the car, which tipped, rocked, and fell over on its side.

The bull went back to prepare for another attack. Quinn pushed the free door upward and hopped out, followed immediately by his boss.

They turned and ran for the protective barricade that surrounded the ring. The crowd roared its approval as the bull followed the clumsy runners.

They reached the barricade, grabbed wildly for the top, and leaped for their lives. The barricade shook as the bull's horns hit it.

Snorting, the bull backed up to study the situation. It took him a while to realize he wasn't going to get these two men, after all.

By now, three other toreadors were in the ring, trying to distract the bull. Another gate had been opened for Herbie, and a policeman was pointing the way for Paco to follow.

"Please, kid," Captain Blythe whined. "Get us out of here. I'm not asking for myself. I'm worried about the lady here."

"How thoughtful," Aunt Louise said sarcastically.

Paco looked in his rearview mirror and saw the bull beginning a charge on them. "Look out, Ocho!" he yelled.

The toreadors were there to help. But one of them tripped over Herbie's bumper trying to get near the bull. As he did, his cape draped itself over Herbie's hood. The bull charged and hit Herbie in the rear.

"Hey, Ocho," Paco said, "are we going to let him get away with that?"

"Yes, you are!" Captain Blythe screamed.

No, they weren't. Herbie now stood facing the bull, bouncing his front slightly to imitate the motions of a bullfighter.

The bull knew his part well. He scraped his hoof on the ground, snorted, and charged.

Captain Blythe passed out. Aunt Louise watched in eager anticipation. The bull charged.

Herbie stood absolutely still until the final second. When the bull was breathing on his headlights, Herbie gracefully moved to his left, and the tiring bull ran past.

"*Olé!*" cried Aunt Louise, and the crowd echoed her.

The bull had one last charge left. He readied himself, snorted again, and attacked. This time, he was coming at Herbie's side.

Again, Herbie waited until the last second. The bull was only inches away from Herbie's left front bumper. Suddenly, Herbie reared up on his back wheels, and the bull ran underneath the car.

"*Olé!*" the crowd shouted, in a deafening roar.

"You can open your eyes now, Captain," Aunt Louise yelled over the noise of the fans. "It's over."

The exhausted bull was being led off by the toreadors. Paco and Aunt Louise were bowing to the cheering crowd. Captain Blythe got out of the car and joined them in their final bow.

Herbie beeped for Paco. Now that the cheering was dying down, Paco remembered how they had gotten into this ring in the first place.

"Pardon, Señora, Captain," he said. "I have to go."

He hopped into the car and slammed the door. Aunt Louise watched Herbie take off for the ramp, as Captain Blythe continued taking bows. She saw Herbie enter the tunnel that led to the street. Then she saw two men step out from a dark corner of the tunnel. One of them fired at the departing car.

"Captain!" she shouted. "That boy is in danger!"

Ten minutes later, Aunt Louise and Captain Blythe sat outside the arena, by the side of the road. They waved their arms frantically as a run-down old bus approached them. Aunt Louise was delighted when it stopped and her niece Melissa jumped out.

"Aunt Louise!" she cried. "Are you all right?"

"All right?" Aunt Louise sang out. "I am ecstatic! I have just fought a bull, and brought the beast to a standstill!"

"It looks like you lost," D.J. said to the captain, whose uniform looked as though he had just been through a wheat thrasher.

"That little car," Aunt Louise said, "is the toast of the town."

"Where is it now?" Pete asked.

"That way," she said, pointing. "You know, I think that boy is in serious trouble."

"I couldn't agree more," D.J. said. "Grand theft, for one thing."

"Some men with guns are trying to shoot him," Aunt Louise said.

"That's no concern of ours," Captain Blythe

said, leading them all onto the bus. "Just turn this bus around."

"That kid has our car," D.J. said.

"I must be on the bridge at seven bells to take the *Sun Princess* out," the captain announced. "They can't move that ship without me!"

"Pete'll have you there in plenty of time," Aunt Louise said. "He's a race car driver."

Meanwhile, Shepard had picked up Quinn and Prindle, and the three men in the plane were searching desperately for signs of Herbie.

"What if he doubled back on us?" Quinn asked.

"We'd have seen him," Shepard answered. "There's no other road around here."

"Just keep looking!" Prindle said.

The three men paid no attention to the bus that was stopped at a service station. The front hood was open, and Pete was trying to make some sense out of what he saw inside.

"What do you think, D.J.?" he asked.

"Beats me," D.J. said. "From what I can see, this thing shouldn't have been running at all."

Melissa was sitting on the ground, reading a

map. "We're not far from San Augustin," she said. "They have statues there that go back to 500 B.C. But nobody knows who made them or where they came from."

"Well, I'll never tell," Pete said.

Melissa gave him an icy look. "You'd probably find a cold six-pack more exciting," she said.

"Look," Pete said, trying to soothe her, "I led you on. I apologize — "

"Please don't bother," Melissa said coldly. "I'll see a doctor as soon as I get home. I'm sure there's no permanent damage."

"Children," Aunt Louise said, "stop this bickering. We're wasting valuable time. Who knows what's happened to that boy by now?"

She went inside to see how the captain was doing. He'd been on the phone ever since they got there, trying to reach the *Sun Princess*.

"Yes!" he yelled into the phone. "The *S.S. Sun Princess*! It's docked in— wait a minute! What's that you're saying? I can't understand you! DON'T HANG UP!" He let the receiver fall from his hand. "She hung up," he said quietly.

He wandered away from the phone aimlessly. His uniform was a mess, his face was covered with grime, even his fine posture had slumped. He looked like a broken man.

"I can't reach my ship," he sobbed. "They'll be worried about me. They can't leave until I get there. They need me so badly."

The sobs took over, and Aunt Louise walked up to him. She put her arm around his neck and drew his head to her shoulder. His crying became loud and continuous.

"I know," Aunt Louise said, "I know. You just tell Aunt Louise all about it."

D.J. had the bus running again. They all climbed in and were off after Paco once more, but they weren't nearly as close to him as the plane was.

Chapter
8

Herbie bounced his way along a mountain road, through some of the most beautiful land he'd ever seen. He rode at a moderate speed, not aware that anyone was still chasing him.

Sitting in the driver's seat, Paco ignored the scenery. He was studying the picture he'd found in the wallet. It was a pretty silly thing for grown men to be getting upset about, he thought.

"Ocho," he said, "why would those men want a picture like this?"

Herbie didn't beep. He didn't have the answer to that one.

Paco put the picture aside and looked out the window. "It's kind of lonely around here, isn't it?"

Beep, beep.

"When we're safe from those men, we'll go back where there are lots of people, okay?"

Beep beep.

Paco leaned his head back and closed his eyes. Maybe he could get a little sleep.

Far above, Shepard's plane followed Herbie's course. It was only a matter of time before the car had to stop.

On another road, miles and miles away, the bus chugged along with its five passengers. It had invented four new noises since the last repair stop, and four out of five passengers were listening nervously. The captain was curled up on the back seat, fast asleep.

"Will we make it to Chiclayo?" Melissa asked.

"Not a chance," Pete said, pumping up and down on the accelerator.

"How long do you give it?" Aunt Louise asked D.J.

He listened a little more closely to the engine's symphony of sound. "About a minute," he said professionally. "Two at the outside."

"Maybe I should alert the captain," Aunt Louise said.

"Don't bother," Pete said. "He's going to be alerted any second now."

And so he was. All the noises the bus had been capable of now stopped. The next second, there was a tremendous explosion.

The hood flew up, pieces of the engine flew into the air, and the engine block dropped to the ground. As a final insult, one of the rear wheels came off and rolled away.

At the sound of the explosion, Captain Blythe jumped from the back seat, without coming fully awake. He began waving his arms and running back and forth.

"Sound the general alarm!" he yelled. "Sound the general alarm! After that, it's every man for himself!"

He pushed his way past the others in a frantic attempt to be first out the door.

"What happened to women and children first?" Aunt Louise called after him.

The captain stopped, looked around, and got a clearer idea of the situation. He tried to regain a little of his composure, but this was difficult, since he was wearing only one shoe and carrying the other in his hand.

"Ahem," he sputtered. "Uh—yes—women and children, of course." He followed the others out of the bus, then asked, "Have you put out distress signals?"

"Right now," D.J. said, extending his thumb, hitchhike fashion. "Five of them, to be exact."

Herbie had stopped at the edge of a tiny town because Paco had said he was tired. As soon as they were parked, Paco climbed into the back seat and fell asleep. He was roused an hour later by Herbie's beep. As he opened his eyes, he heard a tapping on the window. He sat up and saw a man looking into the car.

"Someone wants a taxi," the man said. "In the cantina across the street."

The man walked across the street. Paco got into the driver's seat.

"Wake up, Ocho," he said. "We have to go to work."

Herbie started up his engine and drove across the street. Paco got out, went up the steps, and walked into the cantina.

"Someone want a taxi?" he called out. As a

man's hand closed around his arm, he knew he'd been tricked.

"All we want is the driver," Prindle said.

Quinn grabbed his other arm, and they held Paco between them as they walked outside. Paco twisted, kicked, and tried to bite their hands. But they were too strong for him.

In a large field behind the cantina, a plane was waiting for them. They marched toward the plane, and Paco started screaming.

At the sound of the screams, Herbie's engine started up. He drove wildly up and down the street, trying to find his friend.

"Ocho!" Paco called. "Ocho! Help me!"

Herbie beeped over and over as he drove up and down the street. Finally, he spotted a tiny side street. He turned down it and came out on the field.

The plane's engine was running. The two men tossed Paco inside, then climbed in themselves. Before they had even shut the door, the plane was moving.

Herbie raced toward it, but it was too fast for him. He followed as far as he could. Then he watched the plane take off and fly away.

The five hitchhikers would have given anything for a ride. So far, two pickup trucks and a bicycle had passed them by. When they saw a car in the distance, they all perked up. They were dumbfounded when they saw the red VW.

Herbie pulled up to the hitchhikers. D.J. ran to the driver's seat and looked in.

"There's nobody in it," he said.

Herbie's motor was chugging, and he was bouncing slightly, the way he had in the bull-ring. He beeped loudly.

"It's the same car," Aunt Louise said, "but where's the boy?"

Beep, beep, beep, beep!

"I think it's trying to tell us something!" Aunt Louise said.

"It's a blasted car!" Blythe yelled. "It isn't Lassie!"

"Where's Paco?" Aunt Louise asked, facing Herbie's headlights.

Beep, beep, beep, beep, beep!

"Something terrible has happened to that boy!" she said, throwing open one of Herbie's doors. "Come on, get in."

"I refuse to get into that mantrap again!" Blythe said.

"It's a twelve-mile walk to the airport," Pete said, climbing into the driver's seat. "So make up your mind."

"And hurry!" Aunt Louise yelled from inside the car. Melissa and D.J. were already in. Blythe saw the car begin to move. He leaped for the open door and had to be pulled in as Herbie tore down the road.

Quinn and Prindle sat behind Shepard as he piloted the plane over the jungle. Paco was crouched on the floor in a corner and working hard to keep himself from crying.

The men ignored him. They were busy looking out the window, checking the plane's instrument panel, and glancing at the photograph that had gotten Paco into all this trouble.

"We're getting pretty close," Shepard said. He pointed to a spot on the picture. "Look for this bend in the river. You should be able to see it out that window."

The two men looked out. "What about that?" Quinn said, pointing.

Shepard glanced out the window, then at the photograph. He took a longer look out the window.

"That could be it," he said.

He studied the picture again, then looked down at the river. "The rest of it looks the same," he said. "That *is* it! And there's a clearing we can land on. We should be able to hike from there."

Herbie tore along a winding mountain road, scaring the daylights out of his five passengers. Pete sat in the driver's seat, with D.J. next to him. In the back seat, Aunt Louise and Melissa made an uncomfortable sandwich of Captain Blythe.

Herbie followed a curve in the road, and Aunt Louise and the captain bumped heads. "Pete!" she called. "Maybe you should wait till we get to the track to open it up!"

Pete held both hands in the air. "Don't look at me!" he said. "I'm just along for the ride!"

That drew gasps from the four other people riding with him. The gasps got louder as Herbie suddenly turned off the road and took them into the jungle.

Paco sat propped up against a tree. He watched the three men examining a huge stone disc they had just removed from the top of an Incan temple. It was becoming clearer every minute why these men had wanted that photograph so badly. But now that he knew, Paco couldn't have cared less. All he wanted to do was put his head on a pillow and get some sleep.

"What do you think?" he heard Shepard ask.

"See this?" Prindle said pointing to the disc. "These marks are an example of the written language of the Incas. This stone has tremendous scientific value."

"But is it gold?" Shepard asked.

Prindle hesitated. He seemed more interested in the writing than what the stone was made of.

"Probably," he said. "Pure gold."

Quinn, his eyes large with excitement, asked, "Can we unload it?"

"To any museum or university in the world," Prindle said. "But we'd be arrested on the spot."

"Museum?" Shepard laughed. "University? Come on, Prindle. You're not a collector right now. You're a thief, just like me. We came here to get gold. We're going to melt this thing down and sell it for bullion."

Quinn stood and looked at the temple. "You think there's more around here?" he asked.

Prindle nodded, looking sadly at the temple. "Plenty," he said.

"I say we get this out of here now," Shepard said, rubbing his hand over the disc. "Then we come back with tools and do the job right."

"I guess so," Prindle said.

Together, they lifted the disc and began

walking away with it. Paco got up and trotted up to them. Shepard pushed him away, and he fell into a puddle of water.

"I don't like leaving that kid back there," Quinn said.

"Forget him," Shepard said. "He isn't going anywhere."

The cry of a strange animal startled Paco, though it came from far off. He sat on the ground and decided to give in. He began crying, sobbing in a way he hadn't done in years.

Chapter
9

There was no road for Herbie to follow, but that didn't really slow him down. He bounced his way deeper and deeper into the jungle. He just ignored the cries of alarm that came from his passengers.

After an especially heavy bounce, Captain Blythe screamed, "Does anyone know where we are?"

"I'm sure the car does," Aunt Louise answered. More and more, she found herself saying things like this about Herbie.

"Well ask it!" Blythe said. "I would myself, but we're not on speaking terms!"

"I think we'd better just sit tight," Pete said, turning to face them.

"Keep your eyes on the road!" Melissa yelled.

"What for?" he asked.

Paco ran, but he had no idea where he was running to. He had sat crying long enough to lose track of the thieves. Once he stopped crying, he became aware of sounds he didn't want to listen to. There were bird calls, rustlings of leaves and vines, and once, something that sounded like a growl. He didn't stay around to find out what it was.

So he ran, pushing the heavy growth out of his way, and sometimes falling to the ground in his panic. He never stayed down for long. He thought he'd be safer if he kept moving.

He ran and ran, hoping to find a clearing. It was beginning to get dark and that made him more frightened. Suddenly, a terrifying crashing sound in the bushes made him stop dead.

Something was moving in the heavy

growth, something huge and heavy. He heard bushes and vines being torn away, and a constant rumbling noise sent chills up his spine. Then the rumbling gave way to the most welcome sound he'd ever heard.

Beep.

Now the jungle was lit up like a shopping center. Paco shielded his eyes and looked into Herbie's headlights.

"Ocho!" he screamed.

He ran into the bush and found his friend. He did the best he could to hug Herbie's hood, but there was nothing small enough to wrap his arms around. Herbie responded with a series of soft beeps, intended to tell Paco that everything was going to be all right.

The five riders climbed out of the car. Pete ran around in front of Herbie, picked Paco up, and gave him a bear hug.

"Paco!" Aunt Louise said. "What are you doing out here in the jungle? We were worried sick about you."

"Those men!" Paco said, sobbing, "They are stealing gold!"

Pete put him down and said, "Where did they get gold around here?"

Herbie followed them as they trekked through the jungle, led by Paco. When they reached the temple, he pointed. Herbie shone his headlights on the building.

"It looks like Inca ruins," Melissa said.

"*Si*," Paco said, excitedly. "That is it—Inca. Those men, they will fly the gold away and melt it. I heard them."

"As soon as we dock at Rio," Blythe said, "I'll see that the authorities know about this."

"That might be too late," Paco said.

"Well, what would you suggest, dear?" Aunt Louise asked.

Paco looked at her, then over at Herbie. He ran to the car, climbed in, and settled himself in the well behind the back seat.

"Ocho!" he said, "Find those men and get the gold back!"

Herbie revved up his engine, made a quick U turn, and began to peel out.

"Wait!" Paco yelled.

Herbie jolted to a stop. The others ran and caught up with him. They all got in, and when both doors slammed, they were off.

The three men were in the clearing, but still some distance from the plane. The weight of the huge disc made it necessary for them to stop and rest every few minutes, which was what they were doing now.

"Let's go," Prindle said. "We don't have far to move it now."

The others got up and bent over the stone. Before they could lift it, they heard a crashing noise from the jungle behind them.

"What's that?" Quinn whispered.

"I don't know," answered Shepard. "But it doesn't sound friendly."

The sound got louder. They saw two lights shining at them from the jungle. They watched Herbie tear out of the brush into the clearing. They were all too astounded to move.

"How did they get that thing out here?" Quinn asked in disbelief.

They realized Herbie was coming straight at them, and they finally found the power to move. They scattered in three different directions, leaving the stone unprotected.

They were still running away from it when Herbie reached it and stopped. He lowered his front end, opened his hood, and "bit" down on the stone. Then he continued on through the clearing, the stone held firmly in his trunk in front.

Shepard stopped running and turned to see what was happening. As Herbie took off, Shepard took a gun from inside his pocket. He aimed and fired at the car. But Herbie was already disappearing into the jungle at the other end of the clearing.

"There goes a million bucks," Quinn said angrily.

"Not on your life!" Prindle said. "Let's go!" He led the way back to the plane.

Traffic was light to moderate on the highway leading to the University. In the right lane, a truck piled high with bananas led a small caravan. Behind it, a second truck, piled just as high with the same freight, bounced merrily along.

The third vehicle didn't attract any attention, since it looked like just another banana truck. The difference was that it wasn't piled high with bananas. It was completely covered with them. If anyone had looked closely, it would have appeared to be a self-propelled banana shipment.

Inside, there was a tiny space between two bunches of bananas that covered the windshield. It was enough for the six passengers to get some idea of where their car was taking them.

Captain Blythe pouted as he stared at his feet. "Seven hundred miles on a banana boat with wheels," he said. "I'll be laughed out of the ocean."

"It worked, didn't it?" Paco said, smiling. "The men in the plane, they couldn't find us."

"It was a good idea, Paco," Aunt Louise said, reaching back and patting him on the head. Then she turned to her niece. "How much farther?"

Melissa checked a road map and said, "We should be there in a minute."

The banana car pulled off the highway and made a right turn. It stopped at an information booth at the entrance to the University. The guard came out of the booth to find several hundred pounds of bananas facing him.

He walked around the bananas, trying to make some sense out of what he was seeing. A voice coming from somewhere inside didn't make him feel much better.

"We're looking for Dr. DeMoraes's office," Melissa said.

The guard found himself talking to a banana. "Dr. DeMoraes is in archaeology," he said, feeling as foolish as he'd ever felt in his life. "Don't you want the agriculture department?"

"It's vitally important that we see Dr. De-Moraes," Melissa said.

"Before we start to spoil," D.J. added.

"Stay on this road," the guard said to another banana. "He's in the main building."

He jumped back in shock as the bananas parted. A woman got out, followed by a man in a navy uniform.

"You go on," Aunt Louise said. "We'll get the police."

Herbie took off, then screeched to a stop in front of the main building. Pete and D.J. pushed the doors against the protective bananas and managed to climb out. Melissa followed.

"I'll see if I can find him," she called, as she rushed into the building.

Herbie opened his trunk, and Pete and D.J. managed to get the gold stone out. They slowly began walking it, sideways, into the building.

Panting, they made their way up the front steps and lowered the stone to the ground. They both stood there staring at a revolving door that promised to bring their entire mission to an end.

To the right of the revolving door, Melissa stood holding a regular door open for them. She let them stand there puzzled by the revolving door for a few seconds. Then she put two fingers in her mouth and whistled.

"You guys can do a Laurel and Hardy routine with that door if you want to," she said. "But I think this way would be a lot faster."

They picked up the stone again and moved past her through the doorway. She stepped inside and led the way.

"It's right down this hall," she said.

She ran down the hall, knocked on the door, and opened it. A man sitting behind a desk looked up at her.

"Dr. DeMoraes?" Melissa asked.

"Yes," the man said.

She stepped inside, and D.J. and Pete carried the stone in after her.

"Am I happy to see you," Melissa said. "You'll never know what we've gone through to get this to you."

From behind her, Prindle's voice said, "And what *we've* gone through to get it from *you*."

They spun around as the door slammed behind them. Prindle stood pointing a pistol at them. Pete turned to see Quinn pointing another gun at them from the corner of the room.

Chapter
10

Dr. DeMoraes looked sadly at his three visitors. "I'm sorry," he said softly. "They threatened to kill me."

D.J. caught his breath and looked at Melissa. "How did they know we'd bring it *here*?" he asked.

Prindle smirked at D.J. "We looked for you on the highway," he said, "but we had no luck.

So I gambled that you'd take it either to the police or to the foremost authority on Inca civilization. And I called it right, didn't I?"

Behind them, Quinn went to the drapes and ripped off three sash cords. He put his gun inside his jacket and came towards them.

"Get down on the floor," Prindle said. "All of you. Lie face down with your hands behind your back."

For a second or two, Melissa had some crazy idea about bolting for the door. She took another look at the pistol in Prindle's hand and decided against it.

"You're not really going to destroy that stone for money, are you?" she asked.

"Shut up!" Prindle said.

They got down on the floor, and Quinn began tying their hands behind their backs.

Herbie sat relaxing outside the front entrance to the building. Paco's head stuck out through the sun roof. As usual, Paco was making the most of his situation.

"Nice ripe bananas!" he called out. "Get 'em while they last! Very cheap!"

His prices were too good to pass up, and several students had already bought handfuls of his ripe fruit. More and more passing students were stopping to buy, and Paco soon had a pocketful of change, with hundreds more bananas yet to be sold.

Quinn and Prindle came out of the building through a side door, lugging the stone. Shepard was waiting for them, and he ran to the door when he spotted them.

"Where's the plane?" Prindle said, half out of breath.

"At the end of that soccer field," Shepard said, pointing.

"Go start it up," Prindle said. "We can handle this."

Shepard ran toward the plane. Quinn and Prindle resumed their struggle with the disc.

Around at the front of the building, Herbie drowsed, while Paco went on with his sales. Paco was beginning to wonder about his three friends, but he was making too much money to really worry about them.

"*Gracias, Señorita,*" he said, making change. "Bananas! Nice ripe bananas, right here!"

Shepard was now at the plane, but Quinn and Prindle hadn't made much progress. They hadn't even reached the soccer field when

Shepard started the plane up.

The sound of the engine stopped Paco in mid-sales pitch. He cocked his ear, and his eyes widened.

"Ocho!" he said. "Listen! It sounds like the airplane those bad men had!"

Beep!

Herbie's engine started up, and he began moving in the direction of the building. As he turned the corner, Paco saw the two men slowly moving with their stolen tablet. A fence separated Herbie and Paco from the thieves.

"Ocho, they're taking the gold! What are we going to do?"

Herbie wasted no time. He flung open his right front door, causing a large bunch of bananas to come loose. The bananas sailed through the air and landed right in front of the two men.

They were having enough trouble trying to make forward progress with their heavy load. Trying to avoid this obstruction proved to be impossible.

The bananas splattered in front of them, and they stepped right into the mess. There was a lot of slipping and sliding, and much yelling.

Prindle was intent only on holding onto his

gold. Quinn just wanted to keep from falling into the mess. As a result, Quinn let go, the weight pushed Prindle to the ground, and the disc fell on top of him.

He lay with his face in the banana mush, and he felt it oozing into his sleeves and his pants legs. The stone was pressing down on his back. He lifted his face, and gooey banana ran down his chin inside his collar.

"Get it off me!" he hollered.

Quinn tried pushing one edge of the disc. His feet slipped on the bananas, and he fell face down onto the stone. Prindle's face went back into the mush.

By now, Shepard was running toward them to help. Herbie flung open his left door, and a second bunch flew in the direction of the stone. It landed in Shepard's path, too close for him to avoid it.

He slipped. He slid. He skated. He threw one leg out in front of him. Then he landed right on top of Quinn, pushing Prindle's face into the mush once more.

While they struggled through the sea of mashed bananas, Herbie took off around the building. He found another way onto the field and headed for the plane. He had only one bunch of bananas left, a nice ripe collection on his hood.

The three men were now about twenty feet in front of the plane, the wind from the spinning propellors holding them back even more. Herbie flung his last bunch at the plane.

It sailed right into the propellors. They instantly turned the fruit into a thick liquid which sprayed out all over the three men.

Spitting the stuff out of his mouth, Quinn yelled over the noise of the plane, "I don't care what you say about voodoo! Where I come from, cars just don't throw bananas!"

"Just get in the plane!" Prindle said.

They rolled the tablet through the open door and hopped in after it. The plane began to move toward the end of the field, where it could begin a takeoff run.

"Ocho!" Paco yelled. "They're getting away!"

The plane was moving for takeoff now, but not very fast. Inside, as Shepard piloted, Quinn and Prindle tried to find space for their legs. The tablet took up more floor space than all three of them put together.

"Get us out of here!" Prindle ordered.

"With this extra weight," Shepard said,

"we'll need the whole field to get it off the ground."

Prindle looked back and screamed, "Well, hurry! Here it comes again."

Herbie raced after the plane. Paco cheered him on, his head sticking out of the sun roof. The plane still wasn't going fast enough to take off. It wasn't even going fast enough to avoid Herbie.

Herbie caught up with the back of the plane. It was just beginning to lift itself off the ground. Herbie opened his hood and bit the plane's tail flaps. He held onto them, shaking the plane from side to side. This caused havoc inside. Quinn and Prindle were tossed from one wall to the other, then back again. The tablet rolled in every direction, threatening to crush them all.

The plane finally pulled away from Herbie's grip—and bounced back to the ground. Herbie stopped to watch as it picked up speed. It began going in a circle.

Prindle looked out the window to see what was happening. "Why are you going in circles?" he yelled.

"Because he bent my tail!" Shepard said, near tears. "How am I going to fly with a bent tail?"

The plane stopped, and Herbie charged. He rammed right into its side. The plane went around in a half-circle and stopped again. Herbie charged and rammed the other side.

Now there was a deep gash right in the middle of the body. The plane straightened, raced down the field, and actually began to take off.

But only half the plane made it. The rear, cut off at the line where Herbie had rammed it, fell to the ground. The disc bounced out, rolled a few feet, and came to rest on the grass.

The front half of the plane didn't do much better than the back. It took off, but flew for only about fifty feet. When it came back to Earth, it landed right in the middle of the mush created by its propellors minutes before.

The wheels skidded on the bananas, the plane turned in a circle, and stopped. The wheels collapsed, and the body of the plane came crashing to the ground, its front end tilted to the sky.

Three men came rolling out into the mush as the plane's engine sputtered and died. The men looked up to see that they were surrounded by several police cars.

Melissa, Pete, D.J., and Aunt Louise came

running out on the field. "Paco!" Melissa called. "Are you all right?"

With his head sticking out of the sun roof, Paco grinned at her. "Ocho and me are okay!" he called, laughing. "You should see the other guys!"

Chapter
11

With the sun shining brightly on its decks,
the *S.S. Windsong* sailed smoothly along a
calm sea. It carried five new passengers and a
bright red car. It also carried a displaced captain, who hoped to catch up with his ship at the
next port.

Pete and Melissa sat at a table in the lounge,
talking quietly and sipping cool drinks. They

occasionally glanced over at Aunt Louise, who was standing near the entrance.

She was wearing her most stunning dress, and she had had her hair done yet again. She kept peering anxiously down the corridor, hoping for the appearance of the object of her affections.

"Aunt Louise," Pete said. She turned from the entrance, a little startled. "We're going down to see how D.J. is doing with the car."

Taking another look down the corridor, Aunt Louise said, "I'll catch up with you."

Melissa and Pete walked past her to go out the door. As she went by, Melissa whispered, "He should be along any minute."

"Whatever are you talking about?" her aunt asked.

Melissa smiled, and she and Pete went off. Halfway down the corridor, they met Captain Blythe. In his new white uniform, he was a dazzling sight. Melissa looked back, just in time to notice her aunt ducking back into the lounge. She decided to give Aunt Louise a few seconds to get ready for his arrival.

"Hello, Captain Blythe," she said. "How does it feel to be back at sea?"

There was a slight mist in the poor man's eyes, and his lower lip began to quiver. He looked out the porthole and seemed to be speaking more to himself than to Melissa.

"They didn't know I was missing," he said, his voice cracking. "They sailed two thousand miles without me. All that time, they thought I was in my cabin."

Melissa put a hand on his arm to comfort him. Then she and Pete walked on silently.

Aunt Louise was standing on the opposite side of the lounge when he stepped in. She struck a pose, hoping her dress and her new hairdo would do the trick.

He looked in her direction. His face brightened, and he began walking slowly towards her.

"Gorgeous!" he said. "Just magnificent!"

"How nice of you to notice," Aunt Louise said, blushing.

"I've never seen anything so beautiful," he said, coming closer.

Her smile broadened. When he was right in front of her, she held out her arms to him.

In a daze, he walked right past her. He stopped at a display window behind her. He shook his head in wonderment as he admired the model of an old sailing ship in full sail. Aunt Louise let her arms fall, gave a heavy sigh, and went to check on Herbie.

☆   ☆   ☆

Herbie had been given the best accommodations on the ship, a suite of rooms big enough for him and everyone who came with him. He was something of an international hero by now, and nothing was too good for him.

He sat in the center of the huge room, gleaming with a new coat of paint. His racing stripe and his number 53 had also been repainted, and the total effect was dazzling.

As Pete and Melissa watched, D.J. slid out from under Herbie. He stood up, put a wrench in his back pocket, and wiped his hands on a rag.

"Well?" Pete asked anxiously.

"Considering what he's been through," D.J. said, "he's in excellent physical condition." He looked at Pete and thought about what he had just said. "Uh — I mean, it's ready to race."

Melissa smiled. Then she said to Pete, "Are you really going to let Paco enter the race?"

"I guess so," Pete said. "I'm not about to admit the kid's a better driver than I am. But he *does* get more out of that car than I can."

The door opened, and Aunt Louise came in. She was wearing the same dress, and her hair was all in place. Still, she looked different, somehow. Deflated.

"Well?" Melissa asked her.

"Well," Aunt Louise said, walking over to Herbie. "If I had a full set of sails and masts, I might have shivered his timbers." She patted Herbie's hood. "I hope we win *this* one, anyway."

"Don't worry, Aunt Louise," D.J. said. "This car *is* the winner of the *Grande Premio do Brasil*." Then he called into the next room, "Driver! Start your engine!"

They all watched as the door opened and Herbie's driver stepped into the room. Paco looked six feet tall in his silver flame suit. He carried a bright orange crash helmet under his arm, and he marched over to his vehicle. He stood in front of Herbie and smiled.

"Looking good, Ocho," he said.

Then he walked around the side, got in behind the wheel, and closed the door. He put his crash helmet on and tightened the chin strap.

Herbie's engine started up, and everyone smiled. D.J. walked around to the driver's side and bent down to talk to Paco.

"Paco," he said, "why do you keep calling the car *Ocho*? Doesn't that mean *eight* in Spanish?"

Paco opened the door and stepped out. "Can't you read the numbers?" he asked, pointing. "Five and three are eight. Anybody knows that."

Pete carried a tray of glasses from the bar in the room. Paco took his wineglass filled with cola. The others took their glasses of champagne.

As they all raised their glasses, Melissa said, "To victory in Rio."

"To Old Ironsides," Aunt Louise said sadly.

"To the team," Pete added.

"To Ocho," Paco cried.

And they all drank to that, as the ship bore them smoothly to Rio.